McGEE and me!™

Twister & Shout

McGee & Me! books and videos available
from Word Publishing

Focus on the Family

PRESENTS

Twister & Shout

WORD PUBLISHING

WORD (UK) Ltd
Milton Keynes, England

WORD AUSTRALIA
Kilsyth, Victoria, Australia

STRUIK CHRISTIAN BOOKS (PTY) LTD
Maitland, South Africa

ALBY COMMERCIAL ENTERPRISES PTE LTD
Balmoral Road, Singapore

CHRISTIAN MARKETING NEW ZEALAND LTD
Havelock North, New Zealand

JENSCO LTD
Hong Kong

SALVATION BOOK CENTRE
Malaysia

For Karen Ball, a great editor and fellow McGee-ite

TWISTER & SHOUT

Copyright © 1989 Tyndale House Publishers, Inc.

Word (U.K.) Ltd edition 1990

ISBN 0-85009-286-8 (Australian ISBN 1-86258-096-0)

Printed and bound in Great Britain for Word (U.K.) Ltd by Cox & Wyman Ltd., Reading

90 91 92 93 / 10 9 8 7 6 5 4 3 2 1

Contents

Because the Lord is my Shepherd, I have everything I need! He lets me rest in the meadow grass and leads me beside the quiet streams. He gives me new strength. He helps me do what honors him the most. Even when walking through the dark valley of death I will not be afraid, for you **are** close beside me, guarding, guiding all the way. You provide delicious food for me in the presence of my enemies. You have welcomed me as your guest; blessings overflow! Your goodness and unfailing kindness shall be with me all of my life, and afterwards I will live with you forever in your home. (Psalm 23, *The Living Bible*)

ONE
Beginnings . . .

A tremendous roar split the air. I spun around just in time to see a gigantic bowling ball thundering toward me. Now don't get me wrong; I like bowling as much as the next guy. I'm just not real crazy about being one of the pins—especially when someone is trying to pick me up as a spare!

I dove out of the way just in time—but suddenly the bowling alley turned into a parking lot. As for the bowling ball, well, it was now a giant steam roller! And it obviously wanted to make me a permanent part of the pavement.

I jumped to my feet and glanced at the scoreboard clock. Only thirty-eight seconds left in my "Cream-the-Creepy-Computer" contest. If I could just hold on . . . but who knew what kind of fantastic foe the felonious computer would hurl at me next? Already I had dodged a three-headed Sasquatch, outrun a herd of armored tanks, and talked my way out of eating a bowl of stewed prunes.

Granted, they were only 3-D illusions created by the sinister computer. Still, being destroyed by a 3-D illusion can be as painful as the real thing. Besides, the fate of the entire human race depended on my beating this alien pile of microchips.

You're probably wondering how I got into this whole mess. Well, this space computer from the planet Whatchamacallit (located in the star system Gimmeabreak) showed up early one Saturday morning, right in the middle of my favorite cartoons. Its terms were simple: it would play an imaginary battle game with earth's greatest intellect (that would be me, of course). If it won, we Earthlings would become slaves on Whatchamacallit, being forced to empty their cat boxes and do their math homework until the end of time. If I won, they'd leave us alone and stop making us watch all those "Cosby Show" reruns.

Being the daring and fearless fella that I am, I agreed. (Not that I had much choice . . . those alien computers can get kinda pushy.) So here I was, dashing around the playing field, dodging the computer's best efforts, being watched by a crowd of anxious spectators (including all of the world's leaders and, of course, our beloved president).

I looked at the time clock again. Only twenty-two seconds left! The crowd of spectators jumped to their feet. They began to cheer and root me on. I guess they figured there was a chance of my winning after all. (Either that or they wanted the game to end so they could hurry home and start practicing their cat box emptying.)

Suddenly, there was a loud buzzing noise. I spun

around, expecting to see some big guy with a chain saw. No such luck. Instead, there was a giant mosquito swooping toward me. The critter definitely looked a few pints low and was coming to me for a free refill.

I did what any brilliant intellect and part-time professional baseball player would do. I reached for a nearby flyswatter, took a few practice swings, and waited.

He came at me a little high and inside, but I took the chance and gave a swing. Kthwack! I line-drived that bloodsucker toward the right field fence for an easy triple.

Then, just when I figured I had it made, I started to smell it . . . smoke. Sizzling silicon! It was coming from the computer! Trying to outthink me was more than he had bargained for. The crummy computer was starting to cook his circuits.

The crowd was going wild shouting, "Mc-Gee, Mc-Gee, Mc-Gee . . . "

By now the computer was smoking like a furnace. I thought about telling him how bad smoking was for his health, but I decided to take advantage of the situation instead. I began my own attack. I rushed to the keyboard terminal and typed in the info to create an imaginary supercharged rocket-powered motorcycle with laser guns. Unfortunately my typing isn't too hot. I wound up with a donkey and a croquet mallet. Close enough.

Nine seconds left. The crowd started to count down. "Eight, seven, six . . . "

Suddenly, over their shouts, came the distinct sounds of growling and gurgling. I glanced down to

11

my stomach. It had been a long time since I'd eaten, but not that long. Then I saw it. In a last desperate attempt, the computer had created a gigantic bubbling swamp full of all kinds of squirmy, growling creatures. It was flooding onto the playing field from all sides. I was surrounded. There was nothing I could do, nowhere I could run.

"Five, four, three . . ."

Then my magnificent McGee mind found the solution. A solution that only someone of my superior intellect and experience could find . . . something someone with only my vast knowledge of computers could conceive: I reached over and pulled the plug.

The computer shut down quicker than a shopping mall at 6:00 P.M. on a Saturday night. The swamp disappeared and the crowd raced onto the playing field. They were beside themselves with joy. Once again I had saved the day. Once again life on our planet could continue.

The crowd hoisted me onto their shoulders and carried me over to the president. With tears of gratitude he shook my hand and presented me with the famous Cookie of Honor—an award for only the smartest, bravest, most courageous and most humble of citizens.

I took the cookie, bit into it, and suddenly found myself sitting on top of the Martins' refrigerator. I smiled. One of my better fantasies, I thought with satisfaction as I munched away. But it's sure a lot of bother to get a cookie. Next time I think I'll just go over to the bag and grab one.

Yes, the whole computer contest had been just

the conjured-up creation of my beady little imagina-
tion. Hey, a guy's gotta find some excitement
around here.

Then I noticed the noise in the kitchen. I looked
around and realized that the excitement I had just
imagined was nothing compared to what was going
on in the kitchen below me. . . .

Friday was frantic. Fridays were always frantic.
Come to think of it they weren't all that different
from Saturdays, Sundays, Mondays, Tuesdays,
Wednesdays, or Thursdays—at least not in the
Martin home. No one was sure why. It probably
had something to do with six people all heading in
opposite directions all at the same time.

Even so, this particular Friday seemed even
more frantic than usual. . . .

"Idiot tie!" Dad muttered. He was standing at
the hall mirror and he actually looked pretty good.
He was wearing his new suit, his shoes were
newly shined, and his hair was absolutely perfectly combed. No one had ever seen his hair look
quite so perfect. Not a single piece was out of
place. (The fact that he smelled like a hair spray
factory was probably just a coincidence.)

You see, tonight was a big night for Dad. He was
attending the State Press Awards Banquet where
he had been nominated for a top award. Which
only made sense, since, besides being a great dad,
he was a great newspaper man. But since he was
a little on the nervous side, and since he'd never
used hair spray before, well . . . let's just say he
overdid it a bit. By about half a can!

Yes sir, Dad looked pretty spiffy in his new suit, new shoes, and newly plasticized hair. Everything was perfect. That is, until you saw the tie. Try as he might, he just couldn't seem to get the ends to come out even. Of course, it was all the tie's fault. "What is wrong with this thing, anyway?!" Dad muttered for the hundredth time between clenched teeth.

Over at the table, Nicholas and his buddy Louis (whose mom had agreed, after listening to repeated pleadings from the two boys, to let Louis stay the night at Nick's house) were wolfing down pizza as fast as Sarah could bring it over to them. They didn't bother to tell her that the object of their little game was to keep her running back and forth from the counter to the table as often as possible. Hey, what's the fun of having an older sister if you can't torment her once in a while?

Finally there was Mom, racing around in her formal dress, putting in her earrings, firing off last minute instructions to Sarah.

"Now the number at the banquet hall is . . . "

Sarah had heard this speech a million times and couldn't help but join in: "On the refrigerator."

"Right," Mom said. "And Dr. Walter's number is . . ."

"On the refrigerator."

"Right. And if anybody calls for us you tell them we're . . . "

It was Louis's and Nick's turn: "On the refrigerator!"

Mom shot them a look as she dashed up the stairs. The boys couldn't help laughing. It was a little tricky with their mouths crammed full of pepperoni pizza. Luckily the only ones who had to look at them were they . . . and somehow seeing all that pre-chewed food in each other's mouth only made them laugh harder.

Sarah glanced over to them and shared her always incredible fourteen-year-old wisdom: "Gross."

"I'll never get this tied," Dad moaned.

The doorbell rang.

"That must be Carol and Renee," Mom called from upstairs.

"I'll get it!" Sarah cried as she headed for the front door.

The guys were still laughing (sometimes they really cracked each other up) as Mom came back down the stairs to join Dad.

"This tie is impossible," he groaned.

"Here," Mom said as she slipped him one of those clip-on bow ties. You know the type, the fancy tying is already done and all you have to do is—you guessed it—"Clip it on."

Dad looked at Mom, his eyes full of thanks and appreciation.

"Our little secret," she said with a smile.

"Hi guys." It was Carol, Renee's mom. She entered the kitchen with her daughter and Sarah. "You sure you don't mind having Sarah watch Renee while we're at the banquet?"

"Hey, no problem," Sarah said. "What's one more munchkin?"

" 'Munchkin!?' " Nick complained.

Sarah grinned. She knew he hated it when she treated him like a little kid, especially in front of

15

his friends. So, of course, she did it every chance she got.

"Well, I guess we're ready," Mom said. It was clear she was a little nervous about leaving the kids alone. "I hate it that we're going to be more than two hours away."

Sarah, always the voice of reason and maturity (at least for the last seventeen seconds), put her mother's mind to rest. "Mom," she insisted, "everything's under control."

Mom nodded yes, but it was pretty obvious she wasn't so sure. "I just wish Grandma could have waited until tomorrow to visit Aunt Maria with Jamie," she said.

"Please, Mother, I'm not a child!" Sarah declared.

"Puuuuleeese, Mother . . ." It was Nick's turn to get Sarah. He continued overacting and putting on his best "I'm-a-fourteen-year-old-who-no-one-understands-and-whose-parents-still-treat-like-a-little-girl" voice. "I am *not* a child."

Louis burst out laughing. Nick was pleased. He looked over to Renee. She was laughing, too. He turned to Sarah . . . OK, so two out of three wasn't bad.

"That's one," Sarah said quietly, as if she was starting to keep score. The tone of her voice was clear and steady. Nick had heard that tone before. It meant only one thing: If he wanted a war, he was going to have a war.

"Well," Dad said as he started to usher Mom and Carol toward the door. "It's obvious you kids are going to get along just great." There was no missing the irony in his voice. He knew this was something the kids were going to have to work out on their own. "Good night, everyone," he said as he headed out the door. "We love you, we care about you . . . and now we're leaving you."

"Good luck at the awards!" Sarah called after Dad.

"Good-bye, Renee," Carol said. "You mind Sarah, now."

"Yes, Mother," Renee said, rolling her eyes slightly. Nick wasn't sure, but for a second it almost sounded like Renee had been taking lessons on being a teenager from Sarah. Spooky.

At last the door shut and the parents were gone. Now it was just the kids. For a moment everything was silent. Then Sarah slowly turned to Nick . . . she was grinning.

Nicholas wasn't sure he liked that.

TWO
On Our Own

The battle lines were being drawn. Mom and Dad had no sooner pulled out of the driveway than Sarah started to lay down the rules.

"Now listen up," she said, looking as stern and grown-up as her fourteen-year-old face would allow. "Let's go over 'Sarah's List of Ground Rules.' "

Nick and Louis exchanged looks. What was this all about?

"Number One: don't bother me."

So far, so good. If they didn't bother her, she probably wouldn't bother them. Not a bad arrangement.

"Number Two: Stay off the phone."

No problem. For the past couple of years the phone had pretty much belonged to Sarah anyway. I mean, you practically had to have a crowbar to pry it away from her ear. If she wasn't talking to her zillion and one girl friends there was always that stray boy or two that made the mistake of calling. Poor guys. It's not that she was into dating or anything like that. She was just into talking. And talking. And talking . . . which was what she continued to do now.

"Number Three: I'm not going to spend all night playing referee, so try and act a little more mature than usual."

Nick felt himself getting a little angry. "More mature than usual?!" There she went again, acting as though he was some sort of child barely out of diapers. He started to fire a comeback at her, but she just kept on going.

"That pretty well covers it," she said with a self-satisfied smile. "Basically you just have to do whatever I say whenever I say it. Any questions?" She didn't wait to hear if there were. "Good. I want a nice calm peaceful evening." With that she turned and flounced out of the kitchen.

Nicholas and Louis exchanged looks. A "nice, calm, peaceful" evening? They broke into a smile. Poor girl. She should never have said that. She should never have let them know what she wanted. Now it was simple. All they had to do was everything in their power to make sure she didn't get it.

Their smiles turned to grins. Tonight was going to be more fun than they had hoped.

It was a long ride to the awards banquet, and Mom's nervousness never changed. If she wasn't worried about leaving her hair curler plugged in, she was worried that the kids would forget to lock up before bed. Or . . . or what if they forgot to turn off the stove and accidentally left the milk out and it was too close to the stove and it spoiled and they drank it and they got food poisoning and they had to rush to the hospital and they forgot to bring a change of underwear?

Of course, these thoughts were silly and Mom knew it. But someone had to worry about these things. Since no one else had volunteered for the job, it was, as usual, left to the mother.

"It looks like we might have a storm," Mom said as she glanced up at the sky. The clouds seemed to be swirling and scooting across the moon pretty fast. Dad glanced out the window. She was right. The trees outside were definitely getting blown around. Some were even starting to bend a little.

Renee's mom was also checking out the sky from the backseat. "It is getting kind of windy out there," she agreed.

Dad reached over and turned on the radio. As usual it was tuned to one of the rock stations. Nothing too heavy metalish. Just enough rock to tell him Sarah was the last one to have listened to it. He switched the channel to a station with classical music (something he could never have gotten away with if the kids were in the car).

They listened to something with a bunch of violins and stuff for a few minutes. Then the weather report finally came on: "A good chance of thunderstorms throughout the tri-county area late tonight and on into the early morning hours."

That's all Mom remembered hearing, but that's all she needed to hear. She didn't say a word. Instead she quietly bit her lip and looked out the window again . . . her mind racing with a hundred more "what ifs."

21

Then, in the dark, she felt Dad's hand reaching for hers. Once he found it he gave it a gentle squeeze. He didn't say a word. He didn't have to. She closed her eyes in gratitude. No wonder she loved this man so much.

The kids would be OK. After all, it was just a little thunder storm.

She opened her eyes and looked back outside. The wind seemed to be picking up. . . .

Back at home it was turning into a pretty peaceful night. At least, that's what Sarah and Renee thought. They were downstairs watching TV and Nicholas was up in his room with Louis. They were probably working on one of Nick's crazy inventions. That was OK. As long as they stayed out of the girls' sight everything would be just fine.

Sarah reached for the remote control and changed channels. No sooner had she set the remote control down, then the TV automatically changed channels by itself—to one of those static-filled nonchannels.

The girls looked at each other. That was weird.

Sarah reached over to the remote control and again changed channels. The TV changed back to the static screen by itself. Again Sarah tried and again the TV changed. The two girls were starting to get a little spooked. It was like the TV had a mind of its own. No matter how many times Sarah changed channels the TV would switch back to the static-filled one.

Then they heard it . . .

"Good evening, earthlings." A chill ran through

both of the girls as they stared—the voice was coming from the TV. "I've been wanting to spend time with you two female units."

The girls sat still, wide-eyed and speechless with fear.

Finally Sarah spoke up. "Who are you!? What do you want!?" Her voice was high and a little shaky.

"I am the Supreme Emperor of Probate 7," the voice said. "I have come to tell you that you must start treating Nicholas better. He is—OW! What did you do that for?"

The girls looked at each other. Then they heard a rustling and commotion that they couldn't make out. It sounded like the voice was arguing with somebody else.

After a moment it came back on. "Where was I? Oh, yes. You must start treating Nicholas *and Louis*, his best buddy, better."

Sarah's suspicions were beginning to grow. Already she was becoming less frightened. "Oh yeah?" she said as her eyes began to search around the room. "How's that?"

"You must become his—Ow!—*their* slaves."

"Now wait a minute," Renee said. She was also beginning to have her doubts. But Sarah motioned for her to play along.

"I see," Sarah said as she quietly got to her feet and started looking around the room. "What must we do?"

"You must wait on us . . . er, them . . . you must wait on them hand and foot," the voice replied.

By now Sarah had reached the hallway. She

could hear muffled giggling around the corner. She motioned for Renee to join her. Together the two girls poked their heads around the corner and spotted exactly what Sarah had expected.

There were Nick and Louis, sitting on the steps, holding one of Nick's electronic inventions. Nick was speaking into the little microphone. "Their slightest wish must be your command," he said, speaking in a low voice.

The girls looked at each other again, only this time there was no fear in their eyes. Anger, yes. A desire to see the two "space twits" get theirs, definitely. But fear . . . hardly. Renee started to move forward, to give the guys a piece of her mind, but Sarah motioned for her to be quiet. She looked at Sarah curiously, then followed her back to the sofa.

"What is your first command, oh Supreme Emperor?" Sarah asked.

There was more commotion over the TV speaker. Obviously Louis and Nicholas couldn't make up their minds. They had finally gotten the girls where they wanted them, and now they couldn't think of anything for them to do. Finally the voice said, "You must make them some strawberry shortcake."

"Yes, Supreme Emperor," Sarah said, rolling her eyes in sarcasm.

"And don't forget the whipped cream . . . lots and lots of whipped cream."

This time the girls answered together: "Yes, oh Supreme Emperor."

Up on the stairs the boys high-fived. They

scrambled onto their feet and raced back to Nick's room. This was going better than they had hoped.

Twenty minutes later Sarah was calling from the bottom of the stairs. "Oh, Nicholas . . . Louis . . ."

Nicholas poked his head out of his room. "What's up?"

"Dear, sweet Brother . . . if it's not too much trouble, could you perhaps come down and bless us with your company? We have a little something for you. You too, Louis."

Nick and Louis were out of the room in a shot and heading down the stairs. "Gee, I wonder what it could be?" Nicholas asked innocently. Then he saw it. "Strawberry shortcake!! My favorite. Oh Sarah, how thoughtful, you shouldn't have."

"You got that right," Renee mumbled. Sarah shot her a look and Renee forced herself to smile.

"Here," Sarah said, "let me get that heavy old chair for you." She quickly pulled out the chair for Nick to have a seat. Renee did the same for Louis. The guys snuck a grin at each other. This was paradise. Why hadn't they thought of it earlier?

There before them were two giant bowls of strawberry shortcake. Just as they had ordered, it was smothered in thick, velvety whipped cream. Oh boy!

The girls stood off to one side as the boys dug in. They were shoveling it in so fast that they barely tasted it . . . well, at least at the beginning. Then, slowly, both of them came to a stop.

The look on their faces gradually turned from

puzzlement, to shock . . . and finally to horror.

The girls couldn't hold back any longer. They burst out laughing.

The boys leaped back from the table and raced to the sink. They grabbed some nearby glasses and quickly began to rinse their mouths and spit. For a moment Nick wondered if it was his imagination or if there really were soap bubbles coming out of his mouth. But this was no time for questions. This was a time for rinsing and spitting. And that's what they did . . . over and over again in a desperate attempt to get the taste out of their mouths.

By now the girls were doubled over in laughter. Tears were streaming down their faces.

"What'd you do to this stuff?" Nick demanded between glasses of water.

Sarah could barely catch her breath. "Tell the Supreme Emperor," she managed to blurt out between gasps, "that we didn't have any whipped cream." Finally she brought out the can she had been hiding behind her back. "So we had to use Dad's shaving cream instead!" Again the girls doubled over in laughter. They had won that round, there was no doubt.

But judging by the look in Nick's eyes, the war had just begun. . . .

THREE
The Battle Rages

When Dad finally pulled into the parking lot of the hotel where the banquet was being held, the rain was coming down hard. It wasn't coming down in drops, it was coming down in sheets . . . so thick and fast that the wiper blades couldn't keep up.

"Boy, will you look at that," Renee's mom shouted from the backseat. The rain was pounding so hard on the roof that you could barely hear her. "It's been a long time since I've seen rain like this."

Dad nodded as he carefully inched his way through the flooded parking lot toward the main entrance. "Listen," he shouted, "I'll drop you guys off at the front door and find a place to park."

"What about your suit?" Mom protested. "It'll be ruined!"

Dad hadn't given much thought to his suit. It was his hair he was wondering about. What happens when half a can of hair spray is mixed with water?

"Here." From out of nowhere Mom produced an umbrella.

"Why'd you bring this?"

"I like to be prepared." She gave him a weak little smile.

He didn't notice the smile, though. Instead, he noticed her eyes; they were filled with worry. He knew exactly what she was worried about, too. The children.

He pulled to the curb in front of the hotel. Renee's mom opened the back door, put her handbag over her head, and shouted, "Well, here goes nothing." With that she leaped into the rain and dashed for cover.

Mom and Dad were alone in the car. "Well, I'll see you inside," Mom said as she reached for the door handle. She was careful not to let her eyes meet Dad's or to say what she was really thinking. It didn't matter. He already knew.

"Hey . . . ," he said.

She turned to him.

"If you really want, we can go back home." Dad's voice was kind and steady, making it clear that he wasn't kidding.

For a moment Mom's heart leaped. Yes! That's exactly what she wanted! Go home! Grab her children! Hold them in her arms and protect them forever! Then reason took over.

Home was over two hours away. Just because the rain was bad here didn't mean it was bad there. Besides, Sarah was fourteen. Plenty of girls baby-sit at that age. Besides, who was there to baby-sit, really? After all, Nicholas was eleven. Not exactly a baby. They could look after themselves.

Then there was Dad. Mom knew he'd been waiting months for this awards banquet. He'd worked hard on that news story, and tonight was finally a time when he might get a little recognition. How could she spoil that for him?

"No," she finally answered. Her voice sounded strong and determined. "The kids will be fine." Then, without giving Dad a chance to respond, she opened the door, jumped into the rain, and headed for cover. He looked after her. She was still worried, there was no doubt about it—but she was also tough and stubborn. Those traits weren't always welcome when Mom and Dad had disagreements. But he sure appreciated them in times like these.

Dad put the car into gear and caught himself smiling as he pulled back into the parking lot. He had a terrific wife.

Back home the storm outside was getting worse. It had been raining hard for a while. Now the wind was starting to pick up. The kids weren't too worried about it. At least, not yet. Especially Nicholas and Louis, who had something more important on their minds. Namely, revenge!

Their plan was simple: attack the girls with everything they had—which amounted to one squirt gun, nine wadded-up pieces of paper, and two half-used cans of Silly String. It wasn't much, but it would have to do.

The girls were hiding out in Sarah's room. "Reading magazines," they had said. A likely story.

They were probably up there shaking in their boots—or tennies, or whatever they were wearing—petrified at what dastardly plan the boys were putting together.

The guys snuck up the stairs to Sarah's bedroom door. Then on the count of three they burst into the room with terrifying screams and battle cries!

"YAHHH-HOOOOOO-EEEEEEEE-YAAAKKKKK!"

The girls looked up from their magazines and yawned. Hmmm. Not exactly the response Nick had hoped for.

Then the boys opened fire. Paper, water, and Silly String flew everywhere . . . but mostly on the girls. True to form the females raced out of the room screaming and shrieking. All right! This was more like it! The boys chased them down the stairs, through the kitchen, up the stairs, then back down again. All right! This was living!

Then it happened . . . the unthinkable . . . the horrible . . . the guys ran out of ammunition.

At first it made little difference. What they lacked in fire power they made up for with battle cries and screams. It even worked . . . for about three seconds. Then the girls came to a stop, turned to the boys, and gave them that look. You know, *The Look.*" The look older girls always give younger guys. The look that says, "Who do you think you are, anyway? You're not so hot." Worst of all, the look that communicates that dreaded and unbearable put-down: "Grow up!"

Slowly the boys lowered their empty squirt gun and Silly String cans. Renee and Sarah just stood there, giving them "The Look." Then, without a word, Nick and Louis bowed their heads and, ever so slowly, slunk back toward Nick's room in defeat. How could this have happened? How could they have completely destroyed their enemy, unloaded everything they had on them, and still feel like they had lost?

"Women," Louis sighed. "Who can figure them?"

Nick nodded in agreement. It just wasn't fair.

But they weren't done yet. In less than ten minutes they had cooked up another plan . . . the ever popular and always reliable Remote Control Mouse. It looked just like the real thing and worked brilliantly. The boys controlled it from behind the kitchen counter.

In no time flat the girls, who had been watching TV, were up on their chairs screaming their heads off. It was beautiful. A sight to behold. That is, until little mousy-boy bumped into the leg of the sofa and tipped over on his side. Suddenly the screams stopped. There's something about seeing the underside of a mechanical mouse, with all of its gears and levers spinning, that sort of takes away from the realism.

The girls hopped off the chairs and spotted the boys with the remote control behind the counter. They looked up, gave a helpless smile, and were once again met with, you guessed it, "The Look."

Dad sloshed through the crowded lobby. The umbrella Mom loaned him had done some good, but he was still drenched.

"Are you OK?" she asked as he approached.

"Nothing a good clothes dryer can't cure."

"Well, at least your hair looks great."

Dad gave her a smirk as they turned to head into the banquet hall.

"Oh no," Mom sighed.

"Now what?"

"I forgot to give the kids the Murphys' number."

"You gave them everybody's number," Dad teased. "Next time you might as well just hand them the phone book."

"They'll be fine," Renee's mom insisted. "Don't worry."

"You're right. I'll try to forget all about it and enjoy myself." Mom turned to Dad. "Do you have your acceptance speech all memorized?"

Dad glanced around, a little embarrassed. It was one thing to go to an awards banquet. It was quite another to sound like you actually thought you might win. "What acceptance speech?" he asked.

"The one you were practicing in the shower?" She lowered her voice and suddenly sounded very Dad-like, "My fellow journalists . . ."

A couple of people glanced over and grinned. Dad felt even more embarrassed. "OK, OK," he whispered. "So I have a few general comments planned . . . just in case."

"Well, you should," Mom insisted, perhaps a little too loudly. "You did tremendous work on that story and you deserve to win!"

More people turned to look. Dad could feel his ears starting to burn. It's not that he didn't like to hear his wife's praise. He just preferred to hear it a little more quietly . . . and without the whole world listening in. "Uh, thanks, Sweetheart," he said nervously glancing about. Then, as quickly as he could, he ushered her into the banquet hall.

Back at home, the fun and games were about to end. It seemed the boys had done more than their fair share of attacking. Now it was the girls' turn.

"Oh Nicholas . . . ," Sarah called from the kitchen. "Can you come here a minute?"

"Yeah," he grumbled as he threw open the kitchen door. "What do you—"

He never finished the sentence. A bucket propped on the top of the door came tumbling down—a bucket filled with water that poured all over Nick's head.

The kids broke out laughing. Even Louis. Nicholas was soaked—and angry. So to save face he went into his famous Wicked Witch of the West routine. "I'm melting, I'm melting," he cried as he slowly sank to the floor.

Now it was the girls' turn to high five. "All right," Renee laughed. "We're even!"

"Truce," Sarah agreed. "Practical joke hour is over. We're all even."

"Even!?" Nick cried. How could they be even when the girls were laughing and he was dripping?

"No way," Louis joined in. He was Nick's friend. Loyal till the end. "I'm not quitting until we get revenge!"

"Would you rather have revenge, or brownies and ice cream in the family room?" Sarah asked.

She was an expert warrior. She knew the perfect

time to unveil her secret weapon. Louis hesitated. It looked like she had him. I mean, we're talking ice cream and brownies here. Then he looked over at Nicholas, his faithful, true blue friend. Suddenly there was no question, no more hesitation. Louis knew what he had to do. Yes sir, no matter the cost, a man's got to do what a man's got to do.

"Sorry, buddy," he said as he patted Nick on the shoulder and crossed over to join the girls.

Nicholas stood speechless as Renee and Louis went into the family room to watch TV. That was a dirty trick Sarah had pulled, going for Louis's taste buds like that. Now that it was all over, though, now that he stood there dripping and betrayed, maybe there'd be some kind word of sympathy, some gentle understanding from his older sister.

"Get lost," she said, reaching for ice cream in the fridge. "You're going to warp the linoleum."

Well, so much for gentle sympathy.

"Look," he sputtered as his anger returned. "Just because you say it's over doesn't mean it's over!" It was time to hit her with the cold, hard facts. Facts he'd put off forcing her to see for months. Now he had no choice. "I'm not just some little kid you can boss around, you know!"

"Yes, you are."

So much for cold, hard facts.

"But . . . but I'm eleven years old!" he insisted.

"Nicholas . . . " Uh-oh. He could tell by the tone of her voice that she was about to become the know-everything grown-up, which wasn't so bad. Except that it meant Nick had to play the part of the know-nothing child. "I'm sure eleven seems very old to you," Sarah said as she began dishing up the ice cream. "But as far as the rest of the world is concerned, that makes you a kid."

Nicholas started to answer, to tell her that fourteen was not exactly the summit of adulthood, when suddenly there was a bright flash outside. Both of them looked toward the window. A distant roll of thunder began to vibrate through the house. They glanced at each other.

The storm was coming, and it was coming fast. . . .

FOUR
Beginning Fears

Yes-siree-bob, Ol' Nicky boy and me had some ponderous problems to ponder. When you last left us All-American and incredibly acne-free heroes, we had just gotten a free flooding courtesy of our felonious female foes.

Translation: the girls dumped water on us and got us good.

To make matters worse, they had bribed and stolen away Louis, our Number Three Man. That traitor, that Judas, that Benedict Arnold, that . . . lucky guy to be eating all those brownies and ice cream. Hmm, I wonder what their offer would be for a Number Two Man.

No, really, they couldn't offer me enough to desert my buddy. (Did someone say dessert . . . ?) Besides, this was not a time for weakness. It was a time for strength, a time for courage . . . it was a time to go up to Nick's room and pout. And pout is what we did. After all, I'd come in second at the South Side Sulking tournament last spring, so I was an expert.

How could mere girls have beaten and humiliated us so badly? How could they have stolen our manpower, leaving us so utterly defenseless? And how could they call it off when we were so close to winning?

"Why is it people always call it quits right before you get back at them?" I asked as I sat at Nick's drawing table, ringing out my beautiful golden curls.

Nick was over at his automatic, remote control clothes-dryer-outter. It was one of his better inventions, with all sorts of gears, widgets, and whatchamacallits. He had just hung up his shirt on the clothesline stretching across his room. Then he pressed the remote control that turned the gears and pulled the line until it stopped the shirt in front of the electric fan. Neat, huh?

Of course, I suppose he could have just thrown it in the dryer. But, the dryer was downstairs. And downstairs, as we all know, was "Enemy Territory."

"We need something really big to get even," I suggested.

Suddenly Nicholas came to a stop. I could tell by the look in my ol' buddy's eyes that the creative wheels were turning. Any second now he would imagine something more imaginative than most imaginations could imagine. Any second now he'd come up with . . .

"What about water balloons?!" he cried excitedly.

"Great," I moaned. "I ask for something really big, and all you come up with is water balloons?" I gave him one of my looks. You know, the look that says, "If I wasn't such a great guy I wouldn't

spend my time hanging around you not-quite-so-greats. But since I am such a great guy, I'll put up with your company a little longer hoping that maybe somehow, someday you'll become almost as great as me." You know the look.

"OK, OK," Nick snapped. (He knew the look, too.) "Let me think."

He began to think. Then he began to pace. Then he began to think and pace.

"Take all the time you need," I offered as I brushed out my beautifully bountiful bangs. "Of course, I'm going on vacation in June so you might want to—"

Suddenly there was a tremendous CRACK of thunder! It sent Nicholas through the roof and helped me set a new record in the high jump.

"It's just thunder," Nick commented.

No kidding, Einstein. Here I thought it was some kid across the street playing with an A-bomb.

"It's probably a long way off," he said. "All you do is count the seconds between the flashes of lightning and the thunder and that's how many miles the storm is."

Suddenly there was another flash. To prove his theory, Dr. Nicholas Martin, Weatherologist Extraordinaire, began to count: "One thousand—"

That was as far as he got before it was Ka-Boom time again. Nick looked at me. I looked at him.

"Maybe we should check on everybody downstairs . . . ," he suggested. "Sometimes a sudden thunderstorm can really be scary."

"They would probably appreciate a couple of men like us around." I said numbly, hoping Nick didn't

41

notice my shaking voice.

Suddenly there was another flash and BOOM!

Before I knew it Nick was gone. I mean, the guy split faster than a cheap pair of jeans. As for me, I knew I should be at his side where I could offer my words of wisdom in his time of crisis. So I turned and followed, calmly calling, "NICHOLAS! WAIT FOR MEEEEEEEEEEEEE!!"

By the time I rounded the corner of the stairs, our boy wonder was already down at the sofa, schmoozing with the enemy. They, the enemy, that is, were all watching TV. For the most part they were doing a great imitation of not looking too scared.

"What's your major malfunction?" Sarah asked Nick.

"Nothing," he croaked. He cleared his throat and tried to sound a little more suave. "I heard the thunder and I, uh, I thought I'd check and see if you guys were scared or anything."

"Scared?" Louis asked. "Nah, Nick, we're used to your face by now."

Ho, ho, that's rich, I thought. Benedict Arnold's a comedian now. Then, to my horror, I saw Nick actually smile. What was going on? These guys were the enemy! Sworn rivals till the end! If that wasn't bad enough, Nick crossed right over and sat beside them! He actually pretended to be glad for their company!! It was awful, disgusting . . . worse than eating a health food sandwich, complete with alfalfa sprouts!

I couldn't believe my eyes. No sir. You'd never see me stoop to something like that, no way. I got

principles, I got integrity, I got—
   FLASH! BOOOOMMM!
   I got to see if there's any more room on that sofa!

FIVE
Strolling through Dark Valleys

The awards banquet was going along pretty well—
for an awards banquet, that is. As usual, there
were lots of people giving lots of speeches about
lots of things nobody really cared about. Mom and
Dad were used to that. After all, they'd been living
in the adult world for years now.

What they were not used to was the howling
wind outside. It seemed that every time there was
a pause in one of the speeches the wind got a little
louder and a little shriller.

Then there were the thunder claps. Each one
seemed just a touch louder than the last. Mom
tried not to pay any attention. She tried her best
to relax and not worry about the kids . . . but she
was too good at being a mom. Every time there
was a boom, the knot in her stomach tightened
just a little bit more.

Dad tried his best to concentrate on the
speakers. After all, Mom had said everything was
fine. But just as Mom was too good at being a

mom, Dad was too good at being a husband. Try as he might, he couldn't help sneaking a peak over to see how Mom was doing.

There was no denying it: she wasn't doing well. In fact, the look on her face said it all: "How much longer am I going to have to sit here and pretend to enjoy myself when I'm worried sick over my children?"

There was another boom of thunder. This one was so close that Mom gave a little jump.

All right, Dad thought, *that settles it.* He gave Mom's hand a little squeeze and quietly rose to his feet.

"Where are you going?" she whispered.

"Thought I'd give the kids a call and see if they're all right."

"You'll miss some of these great speeches," she teased.

He grinned. "The price of parenthood, I guess."

She smiled back, grateful for his sense of humor and his thoughtfulness.

When Dad reached the lobby he saw the pay phones were packed. It looked like everybody else was just as concerned as he was. He got in what he thought was the shortest line, but Dad was never a great line picker. Some people can go into a supermarket and immediately know which line moves the fastest. Not Dad. He'd always go for the shortest line. And as we all know, the shortest line always takes the longest.

So he waited and waited. Just when he was sick and tired of waiting and wasn't going to wait anymore . . . he took a deep breath, relaxed and

. . . you guessed it: waited.

Finally it was his turn. He came to the phone, dropped in the coins and dialed. The line was busy. He tried again. Still busy.

"What's wrong?" He muttered, frowning slightly.

He turned around and saw Mom beside him. She had tried to wait in the banquet hall, but anxiety and motherhood had won out.

"It's busy," he sighed.

"Try again."

"I already have." Then to comfort her, he continued, "Listen, they'll be OK. After all, it's just a little rain."

Suddenly the lobby door flew open. As the wind howled and screamed a man staggered in. His clothes were soaked and crumpled. It looked like he had just stepped out of a gigantic washing machine. His umbrella was twisted and turned inside-out.

Mom looked at Dad. Dad looked at Mom. "I'll keep trying," he said.

Back at home Nick was on the phone. He was trying for the millionth time to be the eighth caller to the local radio station.

After he'd agreed to a truce with Sarah, Renee, and Louis, he had tried to watch the movie on TV. But it was just too lame. The fighting and war parts were OK, but all that huggy and kissy stuff got boring pretty fast. He wanted to go upstairs and do something else, but the storm outside was so intense that the tree branches were starting to bang against the house. Not that he was afraid or anything like that. He just thought that if they all stayed together in the same room, maybe they could help save on the light bill.

With that in mind, he had put on his radio head-set and tuned into a station just as it was offering free tickets to "Bleeding Ulcers." They really weren't his type of group. But hey, free is free. Besides, dialing the phone over and over again sure beat sitting around and watching a bunch of lovesick actors get all gooey-eyed over each other.

"Nick, would you get off the phone!" It was Sarah calling out in her always-so-kind, ever-so-gentle voice. "You're not going to win any stupid concert tickets so quit calling every two seconds!"

"I might win."

"Not if you're dead."

"So who's going to kill me?" Nick shot back.

"The lightning, idiot child. Didn't anyone ever tell you you're not supposed to use the phone during an electrical storm?"

"That's right," Renee agreed. "A bolt of lightning could hit the wire and shoot out the receiver right at you."

"Crispy Critter time," Louis chimed in.

"I'm so sure," Nick replied sarcastically.

Suddenly there was a tremendous flash of light outside and a deafening *BOOM!*

Nick quickly hung up the phone. Who wanted stupid tickets to see a stupid group anyway?

Just then there were three loud beeps from the TV and Larry LaFata, the local newsperson, appeared on the screen. He looked a little crumpled and uncombed, like someone had just woken him from a nap in the back room. Maybe they had.

"A tornado watch has been issued for Eastfield and Ashton Counties until midnight tonight," he said.

The kids glanced at each other. Eastfield. That was their county.

"Conditions are favorable for the formation of a tornado," LaFata continued. "The National Weather Service urges residents in these areas to seek shelter and to be on the alert for high winds and flash flooding. Now back to tonight's feature, *Gone with the Wind.*"

The kids didn't say a word. They all just sat there on the sofa. The movie was playing, but they really weren't watching. Wasn't it just last year, over in Rockton, that part of a trailer park had been wiped out by a tornado? Who could forget those pictures on TV of the mobile homes ripped apart and thrown around like toys. Then there were the pictures of people in heavy coats, holding each other, crying, trying to comfort those who couldn't be comforted . . . of search dogs sniffing through splintered rubble . . . of weeping parents searching for children.

It had been awful . . . but of course something like that would never happen here. Not to them.

Or could it? According to Larry LaFata, one of those very storms was coming their way right now.

Sarah tried to take charge. She was the oldest and taking charge was her job—but there was nothing she could say. Nothing to do. The best she could come up with was an offer to change channels.

The other kids nodded in silent agreement. Somehow *Gone with the Wind* was not exactly the type of film they wanted to watch right then. Of course it meant having to sit through the millionth and a half rerun of "Mr. Ed." It didn't matter. No one was paying attention to the TV anyway. Instead, they were paying attention to the wailing of the wind, the banging of the branches, and the pound of the rain as it grew louder . . . and louder . . . and louder.

Meanwhile, McGee was struggling with his own fears. But instead of watching TV, he tried to calm himself down with one of his famous fantasies. . . .

Flash bulbs were flashing everywhere. Outside, the pesky press were packed against the window panes fighting for photos of my famous face. Yes, it is I, Dr. Floss—the world famous dentist, cavity fighter, and superhero extraordinaire. Once again I had cracked an uncrackable case. As I smiled my best "Yes-I've-saved-you-all-again-Aren't-you-lucky-to-have-me" smile, I thought about the job I'd just done.

It all started when Jay Too-Eager Hoover of the F.I.B. called me, begging for my help. It seems their dreaded enemy Nurse Nerveless had escaped from prison and was on another rampage. Her misguided mission? To destroy the taste you and I know as "sweet." Yes, as unthinkable as it may be, Nurse Nerveless had invented a secret formula that made anything that tasted sweet taste sour.

It was a vicious attack on our beloved country. Candy stores were going out of business. Chinese restaurants could only serve Sour and Sour Pork. Even the famous sign that hung in so many American homes was being changed to "Home, Sour Home."

The Nurse and I had known each other for years. At one time we even worked together to fight cavities, stage plaque attacks, and make everyone we knew feel guilty for not flossing. But it was seeing, again and again and again, the harmful effects of sugar that finally pushed the good Nurse over the edge. Seeing hundreds of cavities in hundreds of kids from eating too many sweets was just more than she could take. Her mind finally snapped. Now she lived only to wipe out every trace of sweetness in the world.

We picked up her trail at the local mall. Someone from the Golden Arches called and complained that their hot fudge sundaes were making all of the customers pucker. I hopped in my trusty Fluoride-mobile and got to the mall faster than you could say "oral hygiene."

The Nurse had been there, all right. Everyone in the restaurant was in the advanced stages of puckeritis. Then I spotted it . . . a trail of lemon peels. Raw lemons were Nurse Nerveless's favorite between-meal snack. She had to be nearby. I called security, and faster than you can say "Rinse and spit," they had the mall cleared of all civilians.

Now it was just Nurse Nerveless and me.

That was OK. I knew I was the only one who could put ol' Nerveless out of action and neutralize her not-so-nice nuttiness.

I looked around, then called, "Nerveless?" There was no answer. Only the unmistakable sound of lemon slurping.

"Nurse Nerveless, it's me, Dr. Floss."

"Traitor!" she hissed. I spun around and spotted her above me on the next level. Just as I expected, she was standing next to the ice cream shop. In her hand was the beaker of Secret Sour Sauce. I had to work fast—any minute now Baskin and Robbins' 31 Flavors would be reduced to one.

I snapped open my dental bag and quickly dumped out the contents . . . 1,000 green apples, two dozen Sour Balls, 28 packs of Sweet Tarts, and 5,327 Vitamin C tablets—a treasure trove of tartness.

It was more than she could handle. Unable to control herself, she leaped from the balcony and began to tear into my tangy treats. Then I did it . . . I had no choice. I reached into my vest pocket and pulled out a "Gooey-Chewie" bar—the sweetest candy bar known to man.

When Nerveless heard me peel back the wrapper, she froze. Slowly she turned to me, terror on her face.

"No . . . don't," she pleaded. "I'll do anything you ask . . . I'll be good . . . just don't."

It was too late. I crammed the entire gooey goodness into my mouth. She let out a gasp.

Then I began to chew.

Nerveless closed her eyes, shaking violently. Then she began to cry. To see a dentist fill his mouth full of all that sugar, to imagine what the sticky goop would do to my teeth, was unbearable. But I just kept chewing, making sure the sinister sweetness stuck to everyone of my perfect pearlies.

It was too much for her. She dropped to her knees, begging me to stop. She'd do anything, even go back to prison and dump her Sour Sauce down the drain if I'd just stop . . . and, of course, promise to get my teeth cleaned.

With that I signaled the F.I.B. and they swooped in for the arrest. It was painful for me to watch them take Nerveless away. We'd been a good team in the fight against tooth decay. But even oral hygiene can get carried too far . . . and I knew I'd done the right thing in stopping her. . . .

A flash bulb from a photographer's camera outside my window went off in my eyes and ended my trip down memory lane. Normally I'd go outside for the press session, but I was feeling too humble for that today. So I just pressed myself flat against the window to make sure they got my best side.

Suddenly there was a terrific KA-BOOM and I was knocked back to reality—and onto the floor. I got up and peered out the window . . . those weren't photographers outside, and I wasn't the invincible Dr. Floss. That was really an electrical storm out there doing its best to fry a nearby tree—or a nearby McGee! (Oooh, I hate reality!)

I jumped back from the window and raced upstairs. Not that I was scared or anything. It's just that, uh . . . uh . . . I forgot to brush my teeth after dinner. Yeah, yeah . . . that's right, I forgot to brush and it's important that I be a positive role model. After all, us super do-gooders have to set good examples for you common folk.

So I'll, uh, just hide out . . . I mean, hang around in the bathroom for awhile. Oh, and if it's not too much trouble, would you let me know when the storm's over? You'll find me under the sink. . . . Thanks.

SIX
Remembering God

The storm outside the award banquet was as bad a storm as anyone could remember. The wind was howling and it was starting to hail—hard. It was crazy. To top it off, everybody was cramming into the lobby to use the phones, trying to call their homes, their family, their friends. In fact, there were so many people in the lobby they should have just moved the banquet out there.

A few minutes earlier Dad had given up the phone for others to use. Now it was his turn again. He dropped the coins in and dialed. Mom stood beside him trying to act like she was calm and collected—but it was obvious she wouldn't be winning any Oscars this year.

Dad finished dialing and waited. A concerned look started to cross his face.

"What's wrong!? Something's wrong!" The words blurted out of Mom's mouth before she could stop them.

Slowly Dad hung up the receiver. "The phone's dead," he said. "I can't get through."

Mom felt like someone had hit her in the stomach. What could have happened? Why couldn't she get through to her children!? Before she had a chance to voice her fears Carol appeared. She didn't look so great either.

"It's a mess," she said. "The storm has caught everyone by surprise. The power lines are down all over. Herb from Channel Seven just told me they have sighted a tornado north of Eastfield."

If Dad's words had seemed like a punch to Mom's stomach, what Carol said almost knocked her down. They lived in Eastfield!

"David," Mom's voice was shaky as she turned to her husband for help. "The kids are there all alone."

Dad was nodding. "We've got to find some way to get through."

"Not for a few hours." Carol's voice was also a little unsteady. "The police won't even let the mini-cams out."

Dad let out a loud sigh. "I can't believe this!" He started to pace. It was obvious he was worried, too. But instead of showing his worry in fear, he showed it in anger. "We're at a Press Club Banquet! Two hundred committed professionals who spend their lives communicating with other people, and we can't even get a message ninety-seven miles!?"

"David," Mom urged. "We've got to do something. Will the kids know what to do?"

Dad took a deep breath. "I hope so. There's nothing we can do till it blows over." He was right . . . and he hated it. For the first time he could remember, there was nothing he could do to protect his family. Their safety was totally out of his hands. They couldn't look to him for help. They were on their own.

Well, not quite . . .

"I guess there's one thing we can do," he said.

"What's that?"

"Pray."

Mom started to nod. She was almost embarrassed that they hadn't thought of it sooner. After all, each member of the family had turned their life over to God years ago. Every day they had prayed for God's guidance and protection over them. So why should it be any different now, just because of a storm?

"Pray . . . ," Carol mused. "That's something I haven't done in a while."

Mom and Dad glanced over to her. "You're welcome to join us," Dad offered.

With that, the three of them worked their way through the crowded lobby to a deserted corner of the room. There they began to pray quietly. It wasn't a fancy prayer. Instead they just asked God to look after the children and help them through this dangerous time.

Back at home everybody's eyes were glued to the TV. Once again Ed had outfoxed (or is it 'out-horsed'?) Wilbur. Once again, for the trillionth time, they heard, "A horse is a horse, of course, of course—"

Then another news announcer suddenly came onto the screen.

"A tornado warning is now in effect for Eastfield and Ashton Counties until 2:00 A.M. Several reported sightings have been verified, and residents should move to shelter immediately! Now stay tuned for tonight's Million Dollar Movie: *Summer Breeze.*"

For a moment the kids just sat there, not believing their ears. Then . . .

"We're history." It was Louis. For the first time in his life he wasn't grinning.

Sarah and Renee began to come to life. The rain and thunder outside were louder than they had ever heard them before. "Aren't we supposed to go down to the basement?" Renee asked. There was no mistaking the fear in her voice.

"Great idea." It was Nick. He had just come from downstairs. He was carrying a bucket full of water, which he dumped into the sink. "I checked, it's flooded."

"Anywhere you are it's going to be flooded," Louis sighed gloomily.

"We'll be OK," Sarah said. "Let's just stay here." She tried her best to sound confident. After all, she was in charge. Somehow, though, being in charge didn't seem as much fun as it had a few hours ago.

"I heard somewhere," Renee offered, "that you're supposed to hide in a ditch."

"Oh, right!" Louis smirked. "Take a camera, then when the tornado sucks you up maybe you'll get some great aerial shots of the neighborhood."

Trying to change the subject Sarah suggested,"I think we're supposed to open a window."

"No, open a door," Louis corrected.

"Open two doors," Nick argued. "One on each side of the house."

"Open the refrigerator!" It was Sarah again.

Everyone turned to her. She gave a weak little smile and continued. "I'm going to put away the ice cream." With that she grabbed the ice cream and dishes and headed for the kitchen.

Silence again stole over the group. There was a rapid series of flashes outside followed by a non-stop rumble of thunder. Finally Renee turned to Nicholas. Her voice was very quiet and a little unsteady. "I've never been this close to a tornado before. Do you think we're in trouble?"

"Nah," Nick said, trying his best to sound casual and confident. "They'd tell us if one is going to hit the city or not."

Suddenly there was a bright flash on the TV screen, and what was once a movie was now nothing but static. The TV station had gone off the air.

Louis swallowed hard. "I think they *are* telling us something."

This was about all Sarah could take. "I'm going to call Mom and Dad," she said as she crossed to the phone and picked up the receiver. It didn't take her long to figure out what Mom and Dad already knew. "The line's dead."

Nobody said a word. Everything was silent. Except for the continual ripples of thunder and the constant pounding of rain.

"Don't worry." Once again Nick was trying to stay calm, but it was getting a little tougher to fake it. "The lines are probably just down. The storm will blow over and Mom and Dad will be home."

"Or maybe when the tornado hits us, it'll just drop us off at the banquet hall and save them the trip." It was Louis again, trying his best to be funny. But no one was laughing. Not even Louis.

Suddenly there was tremendous light, like a hundred flash bulbs going off in the room at once. It was so close you could hear the sizzle and pop as the lightning split through the air. The girls screamed, but you could barely hear them over the *CRACK-BOOM!* that shook every window in the house.

After a long moment Renee cleared her throat. "They, uh, they don't have tornadoes where my Dad lives in California," she said.

"Right," Louis shot back angrily. "They just have earthquakes!" His outburst surprised everyone. Most of all him.

"C'mon, everybody," Sarah said. "We're all a little scared. Let's just—"

She never finished the sentence. Not in the light, anyway, for the electricity went out! Renee gave a shriek. The others gasped. Then, ever so quietly, they heard Louis . . . "I *hate* tornadoes."

SEVEN
The Faith Battle

For a moment Sarah, Louis, Renee, and Nick all sat in the dark. It's not like they were frightened or anything like that. A better word might be terrified. Or maybe petrified. Or paralyzed. Or . . . well, you get the picture. Finally Nicholas cleared his throat. He wasn't crazy about taking charge, but he was even less crazy about sitting around in the dark all night.

"It's OK, everybody!" he said using his best Captain James T. Kirk voice. (If that didn't calm them, nothing would.) He got up and started toward the fireplace. "Ouch!" He'd forgotten about the coffee table. "OUCH!" That was the kitchen chair Louis had brought in. This was getting ridiculous. Star Fleet commanders never had to worry about running into furniture in the dark.

Nicholas limped to the fireplace mantle and began to fumble with the box of matches. He managed to burn his fingers twice before getting the third match lit. (This superhero stuff was more painful than he remembered.) Finally the match flared to life, and he reached over to light the candle beside him. With that, he turned around to survey his fearless troops.

Well . . . so much for fearless. Maybe it was how pale their faces looked in the dim candlelight, or maybe it was the way they were all huddled together on the sofa. Whatever the reason, these kids looked scared. Which made sense, because they *were* scared. Come to think of it, so was Nick. But he had to press on.

"Sarah," he suggested. "Why don't you go get Dad's camping lantern from the hall closet?"

She nodded and crossed toward the closet, moving cautiously.

He continued to speak as he headed for the kitchen, "I'll get the flashlight."

Louis, always looking for ways to help, called out, "I'll stay here."

"This is really scary." Renee shuddered when she and Louis were alone.

Louis nodded. "Tell me about it."

A catch started to form in Renee's voice. She figured she was too old to cry, but she wasn't too old to want to cry. "I'd feel a lot safer if our parents were here. . . ."

Again Louis agreed.

Nicholas came back into the room with the flashlight as Sarah entered with the lantern. Setting the lantern on the table she commented, "Dad always says that God is bigger than our fears."

Nick glanced over to his big sister. He'd forgotten about that. To be honest, he'd forgotten all about

God. It made him a little embarrassed. Here Jesus had been such an important part of his life for so long, and now, when Nicholas needed him most, he'd just sort of forgotten about him. Well, that was going to change. . . .

"That's right," Nick added. "At least we know that God is with us."

"Yeah, right." It was Louis. He sounded anything but positive.

Sarah looked over to him, a little puzzled, a little concerned. "You don't believe that, Louis?"

"I don't know . . . I guess." He shrugged.

Louis really didn't know. Oh sure, he knew about God and stuff. He even went to church once in a while. But knowing "about" God and having him as a close friend, well, they're two different things. Unlike Nicholas and Sarah, Louis had never given his life to God. He'd never really asked Jesus to forgive him and be his boss. Someday maybe he would. He just hadn't yet.

"Look," Sarah said. "I know we're all scared, but God really is with us." She turned to her little brother. "Nick, you remember that house we used to live in on Beachwood?"

"Yeah," Nicholas said. "The one with the big basement."

"It probably wasn't flooded," Louis sulked.

Sarah ignored him and continued. "We had this big heating grate in the hallway and every time the heat came on it would make this creaking sound."

"That's right, I remember," Nick chimed in. "Spooky."

Sarah nodded. "I'd lie in bed and just imagine

that the creaking was someone coming down the hallway."

"Our house creaks all the time," Renee offered. "Mom says it's just settling."

"Right," Sarah agreed. "But for me, it was all my imagination. There wasn't anyone in the hall. It was just an old heating vent."

The window lit up with another flash of lightning, followed by more thunder. Outside the wind was definitely picking up. The tree branches were starting to beat hard against the side of the house.

"You know, it's funny," Nick added. "But I never heard the vent when Dad was home."

Sarah smiled. "Neither did I."

Renee joined in, her voice a little sadder. "I never even noticed our house creaked until my parents divorced."

There was another moment of silence. Finally Sarah continued. "I know the storm outside is real . . . but maybe we're so scared because we think we're on our own. Well, we're not."

"So what you're saying," Renee said, "is that God is watching over us right now."

Suddenly there was another flash of lightning, much closer this time. It was almost as if the storm knew it was losing its grip of fear over the children—as if it was doing all it could to try and keep them frightened. Outside the branches banged even harder.

Then it began to hail.

The noise was almost deafening as the hailstones pounded at the side of the house. The roar grew louder and louder.

Louis tried his best to shake off the chill he felt creeping over him. It did no good. "I've seen pictures where tornadoes drove straws into trees." He gave a shudder. "That might happen here."

"It might," Renee agreed. "Or it might blow over."

"Whatever happens," Nick said. "We just have to have the faith that God will help us get through."

Louis took a deep breath and slowly let it out. "You're right," he said very quietly. "I've never thought about it much, but . . . you've got a point."

Immediately there was a horrible *CRASH!* A tree branch broke through the window and sent glass flying in all directions. The kids shrieked and screamed. The wind roared into the house. The rain and hail poured into the room. It was a nightmare. The storm was no longer outside. Now it had come in to attack and scare them from the inside!

Ninety-seven miles away, Mom stood at a lobby window watching the wind and rain. They had called off the banquet long ago. Everybody was just too worried about the storm. Now they were all cooped up wanting to go home but not able to. So instead people wandered around the lobby fretting and worrying and arguing. It got so bad that a fight almost broke out between a couple of men over who would get to use the next pay phone.

Mom barely noticed. She just stayed at the window watching the storm—marveling at its power . . . even impressed by its beauty.

"You're certainly calm," a voice said. She looked up as Carol approached and handed her a cup of coffee. The hours of tension were definitely taking their toll on Carol. "Look at me," she continued, "I'm shaking like a leaf." She tried to smile, to make a joke out of it, but it did no good. The smile quickly faded. Finally she blurted out what she had been thinking all along. "It's been two hours! Two hours and still no news!"

Without a word Mom reached out and put an arm around her friend. "Renee is all I've got . . ." Carol continued. Her voice was trembling and filled with fear. "After Steve left . . ." The emotions crept into her throat, and for a minute she couldn't speak. Finally she swallowed and went on. "Renee's . . . Renee's all I have. If anything should happen to her . . ." But she couldn't finish—the words wouldn't come. Instead, tears silently filled her eyes and dropped to the floor.

"I know," Mom said quietly. "I know."

"Stupid, huh?" Again Carol tried to smile as she dabbed at her eyes with a Kleenex. "I mean, look at you . . . Mrs. Cool and Collected."

It was Mom's turn to smile. "I wasn't that way earlier."

"So what happened? Why the change?"

"I don't know . . . ," Mom started to say. Then she realized she did know. "Remember our prayer?" she said.

Carol nodded.

"I guess I finally started remembering that God loves my kids, even more than I do. I guess I finally started to have faith that he'll look out for them . . . no matter what happens."

"Faith," Carol mused. "You make it sound so simple."

"Oh, it is simple," Mom agreed. Then, with a heavy sigh and a half-smile she turned to look back out the window. "It's not always easy, but it is simple."

Carol watched her friend a long time. Finally she also turned to look out at the storm.

Back at the house it was time for the kids to put their faith into action. The family room window was smashed, and the storm was blasting its way inside.

Nicholas felt himself getting angry. That storm. That stupid storm. They had been frightened by it long enough. Now it was time to fight back!

"I'll get the branch out!" Nicholas hollered over the wind. "Louis, there's some cardboard in the kitchen closet. See if that will cover it!"

Louis nodded and took off.

"Renee, grab the bucket and sponge from under the sink and start soaking up the water!"

Renee leaped into action. Sarah was already heading for the broom and dustpan to sweep up the broken glass.

It was scary for Nicholas to step up to that broken window and meet the storm head-on, but he only hesitated a moment. The storm howled and whipped at his clothes. It almost seemed to be doing everything it could to stop him. Still, he refused to be frightened. He pulled and tugged at the branch. The rain and hail came through the open window so hard that it stung his face. Other branches were blowing wildly, slapping against the broken glass, threatening to break out more

panes. But Nicholas would not give up.

Unfortunately the branch wouldn't give up either. It was pretty good sized and lodged tightly into the window.

"Louis! Louis!" he hollered over the wind. "Louis, I need your help!"

The last thing in the world Louis wanted was to get near that window. He was sure he'd get sucked through it and be given free flying lessons courtesy of the tornado. But that was his friend over there. Besides, if what Nick said about God was true, God would help them.

Louis joined in and together the two pushed and tugged at the branch. It was sharp and jagged and managed to cut up their hands. Despite the blood and pain, they kept pushing. The roar of the wind was deafening. They were soaked to the skin. But they kept pushing. Finally with one last heave they freed the branch from the window, and it crashed to the ground outside.

"All right!!" they shouted.

Meanwhile the girls were struggling to mop the water and pick up the broken glass. The wind and hail screamed through the window, stinging their arms and hands. The torn curtains popped and slapped at them harder than any towel fight. Then there was the thunder and lightning. It was like everything in the world was trying to scare them away. But they wouldn't give up. How could they when they knew God was watching over them and protecting them?

Next the guys taped a piece of cardboard against the broken window. It wasn't easy, especially with the wind pushing and tugging at the cardboard every time they tried to hold it still enough to tape it. They kept at it, though, and at last they got it into place.

As he finished taping the window up, Nick paused long enough to glance around at the others. Everyone was working together like a team. It was great. Sure, they'd had their battles earlier that evening—but now they were all joined together fighting a bigger enemy. And, thanks to their faith and courage, they were slowly winning!

EIGHT
Victory!

No doubt you've been wondering where your adorable superhero has been through all the excitement. Whaddya mean, "What superhero?" Surely you remember me? The good-looking one? Mr. Always-Got-the-Right-Answer-for-Everything-'Cause-I'm-a-Right-Answer-Type-of-Guy? You don't?!!

OK, wise guy (or guyette, as the case may be), just close this book and take a look at the cover. Whose name do you see first? That's right: McGee. Ah, yes, it's all coming back now, isn't it? Good. (I tell you, a hero isn't gone more than one or two chapters and you forget all about him. Oh, well.)

Now where were we? Ah, yes . . .

Where have I been? Well, one of the first things they teach you in Superhero School is to share your glory. You know, to look for ways to help others grow into Superherohood. So, being the great, self-less guy that I am, as soon as that first big clap of thunder hit, I ran up the stairs as fast as I could and dove under Nick's covers.

Not that I was scared or anything like that. I mean, I could barely hear the thunder over my knocking knees and hysterical screaming. I just figured Nick needed to stand on his own two feet instead of always looking for me to save the day. Besides, he hates to crawl into cold covers, and what better way to warm them up than to stay there shaking and trembling all night?

Finally, though, the storm was letting up. Now it was time to go downstairs and check on my star pupil. I poked my head around the corner to see if it was safe . . . er . . . to see if Nick had passed the test. Everything looked great. The house looked great. The kids looked great. I mean, for an amateur the little guy did a pretty good job. Who knows, in a dozen years or so he might even become as great, and as humble, as me.

I noticed the kids had their sleeping bags unrolled and stretched out across the floor. Good idea. After a hard day of superhero action I always like to stretch out for a little snooze. So I headed down the stairs and snuggled in nice and close to my best buddy.

"You did good, kid," I told him.

Nick's eyes lit up like lightning . . . uh, better make that like a nice sunny day . . . without the slightest trace of a breeze . . . and absolutely no rain in sight . . . yeah, that's it . . . no rain or thunder or nothin' anywhere. At any rate, I could tell he was pleased by the compliment. (And why shouldn't he be? I mean, look who it came from.)

"Thanks, McGee," he said with a sigh.

I smiled and snuggled down, ready for the really important business: snoozing.

"Scoot over," I said, "and quit hogging the bag."

NINE
Wrapping Up

The sun had just barely come up when Mom, Dad, and Carol pulled into the driveway.

"Sarah? Nick?" Dad called as he opened the car door and started for the house. He was trying not to run, but his legs ignored him.

The kids heard his voice and were out of their bags in a shot. In fact, Sarah and Nicholas practically knocked Dad over as he opened the door. Mom and Carol were right behind. There were lots of hugs and kisses . . . and even a moist eye or two. Mom held the kids as tight as she could. And the kids held her right back.

"They closed all the roads," Dad said. "We couldn't get back last night. We were really worried about you guys."

"Dad," Nick pointed. "Look at the window."

All three grown-ups turned to the broken window. The kids had done such a great job of cleaning up that it was hard to tell anything had happened— except for the big piece of cardboard over the front.

"Did anybody get hurt?" Dad asked.

"No," Sarah said. "We were on the other side of the room."

By now Dad had crossed over to the window and was taking a careful look at the repair job. "You fixed this, Nick?"

Nicholas nodded. He couldn't help grinning.

"Good job, Son."

Sarah was also beaming over her little brother.

"We were really scared," Renee volunteered. "But we all stuck together."

Carol reached over and gave her daughter another hug. (About the fiftieth in the last minute.) "We're very proud of you kids," she said.

"Yes," Dad agreed. "You guys did better than a lot of the people at the banquet."

"Oh, Louis!" Mom suddenly said and headed for the phone. "We need to call your parents. They're probably worried sick."

"I can't wait to tell them about this!" He grinned.

Later, after the kids had cleaned up and changed clothes, there was a gentle knock on Nick's door. He reached over to his night stand, grabbed his flashlight, and shined the beam on his Light-Activated-Door-Opener-Upper. Of course it worked perfectly. And there, standing in the doorway, was Sarah.

"Can I come in for a second?" she asked.

"Sure."

She came in and stood by his bed. "I've been on your case a lot lately . . . ," she said slowly. She was talking about all the cracks and comments she'd made the night before about him being a little kid and everything. Nick gave a shrug of agreement. What could he say? When she was right she was right.

"OK," she said. It was obvious that she had prepared some sort of speech. It was also obvious she was having a hard time saying it. After a deep breath, she began. "Basically, what I wanted to say was that you were a lot of help last night. I mean, it was pretty scary, but you helped a lot, and I don't know what I would have done without you." There, she'd said it. And it hadn't blistered her tongue or burned her mouth or anything. Gosh, apologizing to your younger brother wasn't so painful after all.

Nick couldn't believe his ears. "You mean that?" he asked.

Sarah took another breath. "Yeah. I guess you're not such a little kid, after all."

Nick's mouth dropped open slightly. Was this really his sister?

She gave a little smile then turned and headed for the door.

"Uh . . . Sarah?" He had to say something but he wasn't sure what.

She stopped and turned to him.

He tried to smile and finally managed to croak out a single word: "Thanks."

She smiled back, then turned and left the room.

It was kind of funny the way ol' Nick just sat there, all stunned like, after sister Sarah left the room. It was like he couldn't handle the change. Sarah actually seemed to respect him. Even more amazing, she'd treated him like a human being! What a concept! Maybe there would finally be peace between them. Maybe life as they'd known it would change forever! And maybe, just maybe, Sarah would let Nick use the bathroom more than ninety seconds every morning.

Maybe . . . but I wouldn't bet over a buck eighty-five on it. Especially considering what happened exactly two hours and thirty-two minutes later. Now, I don't want to rat on my good buddy or anything like that, but hey, inquiring minds want to know. . . .

Sarah was out in the backyard, stretched out on her stomach, trying to catch a few rays. The family had spent all morning picking up the trash and branches and stuff, and now it was time for her to do a little skin toasting. She was ready to rest, she was ready to relax, she was ready to feel that heat bake into her old bones. What she wasn't ready for was a water balloon exploding smack in the middle of her back.

Guess who?

What Nicholas wasn't ready for was a sister who could jump up from her blanket and do the fifty-yard dash—up stairs, even—in 3.8 seconds!

"Nicholas! You little creep!"

"It wasn't me! It wasn't me!"

"Just wait till I get my hands on you!!"

"An airplane! Yeah! I saw somebody throw it from an airplane!!"

Ah, the gentle sound of children at play.

Now, there's no need to doubt that Nick and Sarah really did have more respect for each other. Or that they really had learned a lot about faith the night before. But hey, they're brother and sister. And everyone knows the "How to Be a Brother and Sister" handbook says you're supposed to bug each other. So who were they to go against orders?

Of course, I would have joined in the fun and games—but it was such a shame to see that beach blanket and all those sun rays go to waste. Besides, I had to save up energy for our next exciting, fun-filled adventure. So stay tuned, all you sun lovers and beach bums. Don't go swimming until an hour after you've eaten. And, oh yeah, toss me some of that sunscreen, will ya?

Aloha, Babe.